It's early morning at Prime Fire Station and Chief Charlie is already hard at work, handing out the day's jobs.

"A fire safety training exercise has been set up across town," the Chief explains. "You need to get there first…fast…and on four wheels only. Got it, Heatwave?"

"Remember, you're a robot in *disguise*," the Chief finishes.
Heatwave agrees, excitedly. "Got it, Chief!"

Heatwave quickly races to the scene in fire truck mode, his lights flashing and siren blaring.

He arrives at the Fire Safety Training Center. Smoke pours from the windows of the building.

As Heatwave pulls closer, he notices a cat and her kitten trapped in the building. "Help is on the way!" Heatwave calls as he extends his ladder up to the window to rescue them. "The only thing better than putting out fires is saving lives!"

"Now it's time to put out this fire!" he yells as he douses the flames.

Back at Prime Fire Station, Chief Charlie's son, Cody, reports for duty.
"Hi, Dad! I mean, Chief! Ready for my assignment. A daring rescue, maybe?"
Cody hopes.

But the Chief has something else in mind.
"Washing Sparkplug!?" Cody complains. Sparkplug, the firehouse dog,
wags his tail and barks excitedly. He likes baths!

11

As he finishes Sparkplug's bath, Cody notices a strange smell – it's smoke!

Cody turns to see flames coming from a nearby electrical box. He quickly grabs a fire extinguisher and puts the fire out. "I need to find the Chief!"

Cody and Sparkplug race up to the roof of Prime Fire Station, where they find Chief Charlie.

"Dad! The station's on fire!" Cody yells.
The Chief notices more smoke coming from the stairwell.
"We need to get out of here...fast!" he exclaims.

Knowing just what to do, Cody quickly closes the door to the stairs. "We're trapped," Chief Charlie says.

"We've got to let someone know we're up here," Cody replies.
The Chief thinks for a minute. "I know a way."

Chief Charlie presses a button to activate the Prime Signal and sound the alarm… but nothing happens! "It's not working!" he yells.

"Let me try this!" Cody yells back as he tries with all his strength to turn the Autobot sign by hand.

Suddenly, the sign begins to turn and the Prime Alert is activated!
A loud voice booms through the air. "PRIME ALERT! RESCUE BOTS, RESPOND!"

Across town, Heatwave receives the signal. "Back to Prime Fire Station! The Chief's in trouble!"

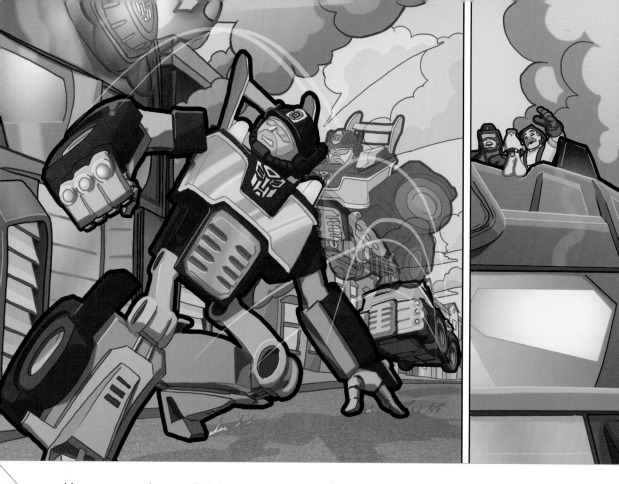

Heatwave arrives at Prime Fire Station to find it surrounded by smoke.
He hears Chief Charlie and Cody calling for help from the roof.
"I can't reach them from here," says Heatwave. "There's only one way to get to
them," Heatwave decides. "I've got to change into robot mode!"

"Am I seeing what I *think* I'm seeing?! It's a giant robot!" cries Cody in disbelief as Heatwave rescues them and puts out the fire.

With the fire safely out, Chief Charlie, Cody, Heatwave and Sparkplug gather in the Communication Room. A robot appears on the monitor.

Cody answers excitedly, "Yes!"

Moments later, the Chief gives Cody and Heatwave their next assignment.
"Is this any kind of job for a hero?" Cody asks.
"I don't think this was in my job description," Heatwave replies.
Sparkplug wags his tail and barks excitedly. He likes baths!